Zoey Lyndon's
Big Move to the Lou

Palmetto Publishing Group
Charleston, SC

Zoey Lyndon's Big Move to the Lou
Copyright © 2020 by Micheal Anderson
All rights reserved

First Edition
Printed in the United States

Hardcover ISBN: 978-1-64111-840-8
Paperback ISBN: 978-1-64111-836-1
eBook ISBN: 978-1-64111-986-3

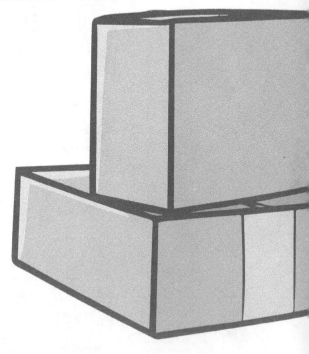

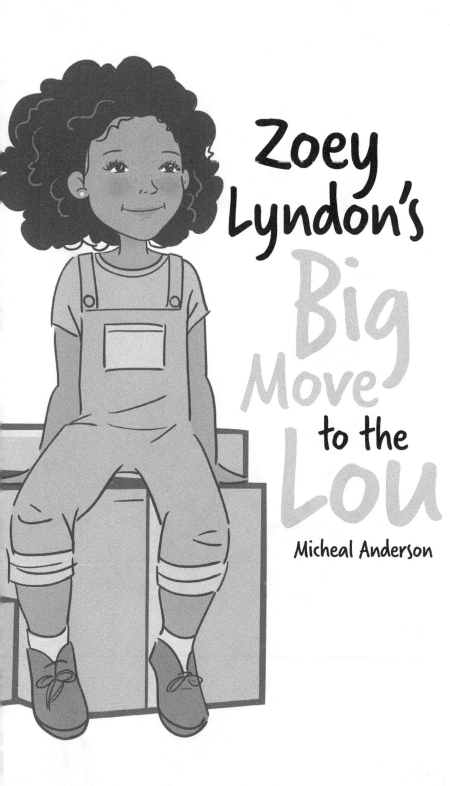

Zoey Lyndon's Big Move to the Lou

Micheal Anderson

Chapter 1

Dreaded Fourth Grade

A ball of nervous energy, Zoey hurried to finish making her bed. Today would be her first day at Briar Ridge Elementary. Fluffing up the last of the pink-and-white polka dot pillows on her bed, she quickly repositioned them before tucking her striped pajamas behind her pillows. She grabbed her pale-blue heart-shaped earrings from her jewelry box and took one last glance in her mirror.

"Zoey, let's get a move on! You don't want to be late for your first day of school," yelled Zoey's mom from the bottom of the stairs.

"Coming, Mom!" Zoey yelled as she grabbed her neon-orange backpack that she insisted on having. She swore to her dad that it would help keep her more organized this year. As Zoey headed downstairs to breakfast, her thoughts were consumed with how well she would fit in at her new school and if anyone would like her. It's bad enough to have to start a new school and worse yet having to do it in dumb ole Missouri. Thanks to her dad's new promotion, her family had to move from Philadelphia, Pennsylvania, over the summer. Fortunately, her mother had been able to unpack most of the boxes and set up both bedrooms for Zoey and her older sister, Jasmine. Zoey was grateful to have all her things unpacked and not be surrounded by any more boxes from the move. Shaking off her nerves, she walked into the kitchen and dropped her backpack at the bottom of the stairs.

"Good morning, Zoey. How did you sleep last night?" her mom asked.

Zoey noticed that Jasmine was already seated at the table finishing her breakfast. "Uh ... I slept okay, I guess," Zoey replied as she pulled out the wooden chair to the kitchen table and sat down for breakfast.

Sensing her concern, her mom asked, "What's wrong, Zoey?"

Spreading some apple jelly on her raisin bread toast, she quickly replied, "What if I can't find the bathroom ... or what if I walk into the boys' bathroom? What if no one likes me?"

"Look, Zoey, I know that you're nervous about starting a new school and having to make new friends. So let me remind you that you are a beautiful, smart, and funny girl who just happened to make it through first, second, and third grades without ever walking into the boys' bathroom. So I think it's safe to assume that you will not start out fourth grade by walking into the boys' bathroom. And just for the record, young lady, the kids at Briar Ridge would be lucky to have you as a friend. Now, how about you finish up your breakfast, and I will drive you to school." Giving her daughter a warm smile and a quick wink, she continued to sip her hot rose-and-vanilla tea.

Jasmine picked up her monogrammed denim backpack and slung it over her shoulder as she got ready to walk to the corner to catch her bus. "Good luck today, Zoe. You'll do great. If you were able to make friends back in Philly, then I am sure that you can make friends here in Saint Louis."

"Thanks, Jazz. Good luck to you too." Zoey said as Jasmine kissed their mother goodbye and walked out the door.

Feeling a bit better, Zoey quickly finished eating her breakfast. After putting her dirty dishes in the sink, she picked up her backpack and finished getting ready to leave for school.

Driving up in front of the school in their blue jeep, Zoey and her mother noticed a lot of families taking the typical first-day-of-school pictures. Zoey thought they looked kind of dorky and was so glad her mom had taken her and Jasmine's pictures at home before they left for school.

"Hey, Zoe, have a good day. I love you," her mother said as Zoey grabbed her neon backpack and stepped out of the jeep.

"Thanks, Mom. Love you too," she replied just before closing the car door and heading into the unknown of Briar Ridge Elementary.

Zoey found her classroom with no trouble at all. She noticed that it was only three doors down from the girls' restroom. She inwardly smiled as she walked into her classroom thinking, *At least I don't have to worry about walking into the boy's restroom now.* She couldn't help but notice how excited everyone seemed to be. She wondered if she was the only one who was nervous about the first day of school. She noticed how friendly her teacher seemed as she smiled and greeted her students.

"Good morning, class" she said cheerily. "Welcome to the fourth grade! Please come in and find your seat. My name is Mrs. Pennington. I am so glad to have each of you in my class for this year."

Zoey thought Mrs. Pennington seemed real nice. She thought Mrs. Pennington must have pretty good style too, because Zoey especially liked her teacher's white poofy skirt with all the little cherries on it. Mrs. Pennington went over the basic classroom housekeeping stuff first. She took attendance, passed out fifty million papers that needed to go home to be completed by the kids' parents, and told them the forms must be returned the next day. Afterward, she gave her class a choice of how they could address her—either Mrs. Penni or Mrs. P. The class decided on Mrs. P.

Most of the morning, Mrs. P. had her students introduce themselves and talk briefly about what they had done over the summer. In the afternoon Mrs. P. actually taught a math lesson and gave out homework. Zoey thought that this was the longest day ever, and who in the heck gives out math homework on the first day of school? Right before school was getting ready to let out, Mrs. P. gave everyone a list of the school clubs and activities they could participate in. At 3:00, the bell rang. Zoey sighed and thought, *Finally, it's time to go home.* Packing up her things and throwing her neon-orange backpack across her right shoulder, she headed out the door.

Mrs. P. said, "Miss Zoey, it was a pleasure to have you in class today! I know that you are new to town, but I think you will find that there is a lot to do in the Lou."

Zoey's hazel-colored eyes showed her confusion as she asked, "What's the Lou?"

Mrs. P. chuckled and said, "The Lou is how we affectionately refer to Saint Louis." She gave Zoey a warm smile and said, "See you tomorrow."

"Oh, I get it. That is kind of like how we refer to Philadelphia as Philly. Right?"

Smiling, Mrs. P. replied, "That sounds about right."

"See you tomorrow, Mrs. P.," Zoey delightedly replied as she smiled and waved back at Mrs. P., and then she headed home.

As Zoey walked into the house and dropped her backpack in the corner of the hallway, she asked her mom, "Is Jasmine home yet?"

"Yes, Jasmine has been home for almost a half hour. She's in the kitchen having a snack. Take your backpack upstairs to your room and then you can have a snack before dinner."

"Sure, Mom," Zoey said as she grabbed her backpack and headed upstairs to drop it in her bedroom.

"So how did it go today?" asked Jasmine as Zoey entered the kitchen for a snack.

Opening the cabinet, Zoey got a bowl and then opened the refrigerator and grabbed a handful of the big green seedless grapes. "My day was so boring. I like my old school better."

"Well, of course you do, silly! That's only natural because you haven't made any new friends yet."

"I don't think anyone likes me," replied Zoey. "No one talked to me all day, and I had to eat lunch by myself. It was horrible! I hate Missouri. I mean, even the name sounds like you're saying misery."

Sitting with her arms crossed and leaning back in her chair, Jasmine belted out a laugh. "Oh my God! I was thinking the same thing. That is so funny that you said that." Jasmine chuckled and asked, "Well, did you talk to anyone today or try to sit with anyone at lunchtime?"

"I tried to sit with a girl in my class at lunch, but she told me that she was saving seats for her friends. After that I decided to just sit by myself."

Jasmine could tell by the sad look in Zoey's eyes that her sister's first day of school hadn't gone very well. "You should look into joining a club so that you can make some new friends."

"I don't know what clubs to join." Zoey answered.

"Today I met this girl, Aubrey, in my class, and we decided to join both the Drama Club and the Tennis Club. But I need Mom to fill out some forms."

Zoey remembered her new teacher, Mrs. Pennington—Mrs. P. for short—had given her class a list of clubs and activities too. She hurried upstairs to find it. Hopeful at the possibility of making friends, she reviewed the list before getting started on her homework. When her mother passed by her room, she called out to her, "Hey Mom! I have some forms for you and Dad to sign!"

Her mother stepped inside her room. "What are they?"

"Mrs. P. says we need to return them all tomorrow."

Her mom looked over the papers and then returned her gaze to Zoey. "How was school today? Did you make any new friends?"

With a long face, Zoey said, "No, not really, but Jasmine suggested I sign up for a club or activity to help me make new friends."

"Ah, so these are very important then." Her mom sat the forms beside Zoey on her bed. "But it looks like you haven't selected a club yet."

"I know, I know, Mom. I just wanted to make sure I gave you the forms now so that you don't forget."

"I won't forget … and I agree with Jasmine, I think this is a great way to get involved and meet new people at school."

Zoey nodded her head in agreement as her mom stood to leave.

"I'll let you get back to it then." Her mom said as she exited Zoey's room.

Zoey laid back on her bed with her ankles crossed. She held the list over her head. The Anime Club sounded interesting. She and her sister both enjoyed anime. *Hmm… Comic Book Club, Pokémon Club, Zombie Survival Club—I will definitely not be joining any zombie club.* She turned over onto her belly. *Free Hug Club … that is definitely going to be a NO! Chess Club,*

Newspaper Club, Math Club, Cup Stacking Club...

"What the heck is a Cup Stacking Club?" she said aloud. She tried to figure out what someone would do in a cup stacking club and then decided she didn't want to know. *Science Club.* Hmm ... she loved science. "Yup, this might just work."

The thought of making friends through the Anime Club and Science Club made her feel a lot better. Maybe Briar Ridge wouldn't be so bad after all.

Later that evening, after Zoey got ready for bed, she told her dad about all the clubs her new school offered as he sat on the foot of her bed.

"So, which do you want to join?" he asked.

"I'm thinking about joining either the Anime or Science Club."

"You've always liked science, baby girl, so I think that would be a great choice for you."

"Yeah, Daddy, but it seems like the Anime Club might be more popular and there are probably not that many girls in the Science Club anyway."

Leaning back and cocking his head to the side to show his surprise, her father asked, "Since when do you care about being popular? Baby girl, you can join whatever club you like, but make sure you're joining it for the right reason and not just because it's popular."

"Okay, Daddy," she said, nodding her head in agreement. She just wasn't so sure that his advice would help her make new friends.

Letting out a big yawn and stretching her arms, she asked, "So how was your day, Daddy?"

He chuckled and said, "Looks like someone is getting sleepy. My day was fine. I'm just sorry that I couldn't be home to see you and Jasmine off to school this morning."

She gave her dad a sleepy smile and squeezed his hand "Oh, Daddy ... we know you couldn't be here this morning because of your new job. Mom made sure we took plenty of first-day pictures. We all know how you like your first-day-of-school photos," she said exaggeratedly.

"Well, that's good to hear," her father said as he stood up and leaned over to kiss her good night.

ZOEY LYNDON'S BIG MOVE TO THE LOU

"Sleep tight, baby girl," he told her as he headed to her sister's room to say good night to her.

Chapter 2

Cafeteria Blues

The next morning Mrs. P. was standing at the door of the classroom greeting her students with a bright smile. "Good morning, Miss Zoey. I really like your backpack." Mrs. P. greeted Zoey as she entered the classroom.

Zoey, impressed that Mrs. P. remembered her name, smiled and said, "Thanks, Mrs. P."

She entered the classroom and quickly found her seat. Mrs. P. walked to the front of the classroom to greet her students. "Good morning, class. Before we get started today, I need to collect everyone's school forms that your parents should have completed last night." She asked everyone to pass their form folders forward and collected them from the first student in each row. "Any student who forgot to bring in your completed forms today, please make sure you bring them in tomorrow. I noticed that we have a few new students who are new to Briar Ridge.

"Before we get started on our math homework, does anyone have questions about any of the clubs and activities that we offer?"

Several kids held up their hands to ask questions and talk about how much fun the different clubs were. Zoey raised her hand, too, and when Mrs. P. called her name, Zoey told her that she was interested in signing up for the Science Club. Then she asked, "How often do we meet?"

Mrs. P. smiled, standing with her right hand in the pocket of her pink-and-white checkerboard skirt. "That's great, Zoey. I'm actually in charge of the school's science club, and we meet once every two weeks on Wednesdays. There is also an opportunity to participate in two different science fairs for the school year. One is held by the school, and the other is held by the school district. The one held by the district is open to all the elementary schools in the school district."

"Thank you, Mrs. P." Zoey decided to take her father's advice and join the club that she knew would be the best fit for her. She had always loved science and knew that the Anime Club wasn't going to be the right club for her.

Mrs. P. agreed to take only a few more questions before asking her class to take out their math homework. "Class, I want you to switch your homework with the person sitting behind you, and if you are in the last row, exchange your paper with the person sitting to your right."

Just then a girl with the biggest almond-shaped brown eyes Zoey had ever seen raised her hand and said, "Mrs. P., I don't have anyone sitting to my right."

"Tomasina, you can switch with Lou." He was the boy sitting directly in front of her.

Zoey took a pencil out of her pencil case, and the boy next to her, whose name was Jackson Smith, asked, "Can I please borrow a pencil?"

"Sure!" Quickly reaching into her pencil case, she grabbed another pencil and handed it to him.

Jackson gave her a big ole toothy grin before he took the pencil and said, "Thanks a lot."

Just then the girl sitting behind Zoey tapped her shoulder and whispered, "You probably won't want that back. Jackson likes to put pencils in his nose."

"Eww! That is gross!" she said under her breath as she frowned up her face.

Mrs. P. went through each math problem, and as Zoey checked each of Josh Hightower's answers, she also had Jackson Smith in her peripheral view, trying to see if what the girl behind her said was true. Sure enough, by the time Mrs. P. got to the eighth question, Zoey saw Jackson slide the eraser top of the pencil up his nose! Her eyes widened as big as saucers. She was so mad! Inwardly kicking herself, she thought, *Why did I give him my pencil? Who does that?* She decided that she would just tell him that he could keep it if he tried to give it back.

Mrs. P. finished reviewing all twelve math problems, and Josh Hightower got them all correct, so Zoey gave him a smiley face before returning his homework. She turned around and got her homework back from the girl who sat behind her. She had written a big fat 100 percent on Zoey's homework. Trying to hide her irritation about the girl marking up the whole top of her homework, she smiled and said, "Thank you."

With a little wicked grin, and a little too much enthusiasm, the girl seated behind her said "Told ya!" She looked over at Jackson before turning back around in her seat. Zoey wasn't smiling.

Mrs. P. covered another math lesson and a reading lesson, and she took her class to visit the library before it was time for lunch. Zoey was starting to get hungry and was ready for lunch. Yesterday she had ended up sitting alone because when she asked a classmate if she could sit with her, the girl told her no, because she was saving the seats for her friends. She felt embarrassed and was hoping that today would be different.

She prepared to go to the dreaded cafeteria. Since Zoey packed her lunch, she was allowed to sit down while most of her classmates went through the cafeteria line because they were buying the school lunch. Zoey sat down at the end of the table and opened up her lunch box.

She had a turkey-and-cheese sandwich, pretzels, sliced apples, and a small bottle of hot sauce. She liked spicy food and wouldn't eat her turkey sandwich without hot sauce, so she had talked her mom into getting her a small bottle. She decided to take out the book that she was reading, *Mackenzie Blue: The Secret Crush*, and placed it next to her lunch box on the cafeteria table. She started to eat her lunch and watched as her classmates began to take their seats with their friends. She waited to see if anyone would sit with her today, and after waiting a few more minutes, she realized that she would be sitting alone again. She added a few more drops of hot sauce to her sandwich and finished eating her lunch. Grateful that she had bought her book, she picked it up and said under her breath, "Thank God I remembered to bring my book." Opening it up to chapter 7, titled "The New Girl (and Boy)," she began eating her sliced apples.

That afternoon, Mrs. P. talked about the school science fair and asked, "If anyone would like to participate in the science fair, please let me know, and I will give you a packet that explains the guidelines for all participants.

Participation is not mandatory, but students who do participate will receive extra credit. Those students who do not participate will be able to support your classmates who are choosing to participate." Mrs. P. said, "The science fair is in six weeks, and if anyone needs help selecting a project, please see me after school."

Immediately, the wheels in Zoey's head started to spin while she thought of what type of project she could do. She raised her hand so that Mrs. P. would give her the science fair guidelines packet. Zoey told her, "Thank you. I will read over it tonight."

"Sure, and let me know if you have any questions, Zoey, or if you need any help with selecting a project."

Mrs. P. went over a social studies lesson that afternoon and talked about the American Revolution. She seemed to really enjoy talking about the British government fighting with the Colonial government, about taxes and free trade. Zoey, trying to not let her eyes glaze over from boredom, stayed focused. Mrs. P. instructed the class to finish reading the chapter for homework because it was time to pack up and get ready to go home.

While she was packing up her backpack, Jackson Smith handed Zoey her pencil back and said, "Here's your pencil back."

"Uh ... that's okay. You can keep it in case you need it tomorrow."

Smiling, he asked, "You sure?"

She nodded and said, "Yeah, I'm sure."

"Thanks, Zoey!"

Zoey headed out to her mom's car thinking there was no way she was going to take that pencil back! And she wondered, *Why in the heck was he smiling at me like a Cheshire cat?*

Tonight was Taco Tuesday in the Lyndon household, and Zoey and Jasmine loved making their own tacos and eating Spanish rice. Her dad asked the girls how their day at school was, and Jasmine excitedly told him, "My day was good. Aubrey and I are going to join the Tennis Club, and I have the permission slip that you have to sign, Daddy."

"Since when did you start liking tennis?" Dad asked Jasmine, and he took a bite of his second taco.

"Dadddddy ... you are always telling us to try new things," Jasmine said.

Her mom chimed in and said, "Let the girl play tennis if she wants to, David."

Dad laughed and with humor in his eyes said, "Aww Rachel ... Jasmine knows I'm only teasing her!" He gave his wife an exaggerated wink.

"So how did things go for you today, Zoe?" Her Mom asked.

Starting to feel like a misfit, Zoey was embarrassed to let her mother know that she wasn't making friends and had been eating lunch alone. "Mom, I don't really like my new school ... and I miss my old friends," she griped as she added more taco sauce to her hard-shell taco.

"Well, how do the kids seem in class?" her mom asked.

Jasmine blurted, "Zoey has been eating lunch alone and doesn't want to ask the other girls if she can eat with them!"

"Is this true, Zoe?" Her dad asked.

Zoey rolled her eyes at her sister and snapped, "Jasmine, why do you always gotta tell my business?"

"Young lady, you are entirely too young to have any business," her father said in a firm voice that let Zoey know he meant business and she better not try him.

"Now answer the question," he said.

"Yeah, Daddy, it's true," she said, dropping her head just a smidge while still giving Jasmine the evil eye. "I did try, though, Daddy." Zoey exclaimed. "Yesterday I asked a girl in my class if I could sit with her, and she told me no, because she was saving the seats for her friends."

"I understand that you girls are in a new city, new home, new school, and you miss your old friends. I really want you to give your new school a chance," he said, looking at both girls. "Zoey, you have an amazing wit, and you are supersmart! So tomorrow when you go to school, I want you to introduce yourself to at least one girl in your class and show them who you are," he said as he gave her a reassuring smile.

"Zoe, I am in the same boat as you right now, because I miss my friends, and I have to make new friends too. Making friends is not always easy to do, especially when you are in a new city and school. Sometimes just having an ally can make all the difference," her mom told her as she gave Zoey a reassuring smile of encouragement.

Zoey asked, "What is an ally?"

"An ally is someone who supports you or someone who is in your corner," her mom said.

Her dad said, "Everyone needs an ally in their life at some point. Promise me that you will give your school a chance before you decide if you like it or not."

Zoey nodded her head and reluctantly said, "Okay, Daddy, I will."

Her mom smiled at her, and her dad said, "That's all we ask, baby girl."

Changing the subject, Mom asked, "So who has cleanup?"

As if on cue, both girls sighed in unison, got up, and started clearing the dishes and cleaning the kitchen.

Chapter 3

Things Are Looking Up

The next day in school, Zoey remembered what she had promised her dad—that she would introduce herself to at least one girl today. The day was already half over, and she had not had the time to follow through on her promise yet. Since today was Wednesday, they had a Science Club meeting after school, and maybe there would be a girl who seemed nice that she could introduce herself to if she didn't get to do it before then. She was secretly dreading this for some reason and didn't know why.

At lunch, as usual, the kids who packed their lunches got to find seats first, and the kids who bought the school lunch had to stand in line. Zoey sat in her usual seat and pulled out her turkey-and-cheese sandwich, pretzels, apple slices, and the small bottle of hot sauce, then began to eat her lunch. As the other kids walked by, she tried to appear friendly and smile. Some spoke and smiled back but continued past her to sit with their friends. Letting out a big sigh, she reached for her book thinking, *I hate this school, and I hate Saint Louis.*

"Do you mind if I sit here?"

Zoey looked up, and with her fingers still gripping her book, she replied, "No, I don't mind."

"Hi. My name is Tomasina, but everyone calls me Tommi."

"Hi. I'm Zoey."

"Yeah, I know. You just moved here, right?"

"Yeah, I'm the new girl," she said, smiling.

"Where did you move from?" Tommi asked as she placed her lunch tray and water bottle in front of her.

"We moved here from Philly."

"Where is that?" Tommi asked.

Zoey chuckled before she replied, "Philadelphia, Pennsylvania."

"Oh!" Tommi nodded her head in acknowledgment. "So, what do you think of Briar Ridge so far?"

Zoey thought for a moment and decided to play it safe. "It's pretty nice so far. I like Mrs. P., and the Science Club sounds pretty interesting."

"Yeah, we lucked out with Mrs. P.! She's the best fourth-grade teacher. All the students want to be in her class." Tommi asked her, "Didn't you join the Science Club?"

"Yes, I did. Science is one of my favorite subjects."

"Mine too!" Tommi exclaimed and then asked abruptly asked, "Hey, is that a bottle of hot sauce?"

Zoey realized she had forgotten to put it back in her lunch box after using it for her turkey sandwich. Wondering where this was headed, she replied, "Yes, it is. I won't eat my turkey sandwich unless I have hot sauce on it."

Tommi gave her a sly little grin and said, "Ooh, girl, can I have some?"

"Sure," Zoey smiled and let out a small sigh of relief before handing her the bottle.

Tommi sprinkled a few drops on the remainder of her chicken sandwich and gave the bottle back to Zoey before saying, "Thanks, Zoey!"

As Tommi took another bite of her sandwich, she said, "I guess I'll see you after school, since today's our first Science Club meeting."

"You sure will," said Zoey as she packed up her lunch box to get ready to head back to their classroom.

"I told my mom that we had a new girl in class and that you seemed real nice. She said I should introduce myself to you, especially since I was the new girl last year!" she said, smiling at Zoey.

"Really?" said Zoey.

"Oh yeah! I started halfway through third grade, and I remember how hard it was to make friends. I was sooo mad at my mom and dad!"

"Were you mad because you had to move?"

"No. My parents were getting a divorce, and me and my mom moved because of that."

"Oh, I'm sorry. I didn't mean to be nosy," she said genuinely.

"Nah, it's okay. My dad ended up moving here too, so I still get to see him. I just wish we all still lived together."

Zoey instantly regretted asking the question and wasn't sure how she should respond. She gave her a sympathetic smile and said, "I think it's time to go back to class." Zoey had enjoyed talking to Tommi and thought she seemed really nice. She didn't have any friends whose parents were divorced and could tell that talking about it made Tommi a little sad. She was looking forward to talking to her some more to see what else they might have in common other than science and hot sauce. She was also curious to see what science project she would work on in the Science Club.

After school, the students met in the cafeteria for the Science Club. Zoey saw Tommi and walked over to sit with her. She was already sitting with another girl and Josh Hightower from class. Today the students had to tell Mrs. P. what science project they were planning on submitting for the science fair. Mrs. P. went over the club expectations and reminded everyone that they should do most of the work for their projects and not their parents. She then asked each student what their projects were, and there were a lot of interesting projects. Mrs. P. then asked Zoey what she was planning on doing for her project.

Zoey said, "Ohm's law."

"Oh, that sounds interesting! I think that's a good choice," she said with an approving smile and quick nod of her head.

Tommi's project was edible DNA, and Josh Hightower's was growing crystals. There were a couple of people who hadn't picked a project, and Mrs. P. gave them an extra two days to finalize their projects. When the Science Club meeting was over, everyone packed up to go home. They were all excited and couldn't wait to get started on their projects.

Later that evening after Jasmine and Zoey had finished their homework, Jasmine went out to the garage. Her dad had just pulled out the lawnmower to cut the grass.

"Daddy, do you mind if Zoey and I ride our bikes over to Aubrey's house?"

"Are you girls done with your homework?"

"Yeah," they answered in unison.

"Okay then, but make sure you are back by seven o'clock on the dot. And make sure you give your mother your friend's address."

"I already did!" Jasmine said. As the girls went off on their bikes, they waved and yelled back, "See ya, Daddy!"

As the girls peddled their way down Wrenwood Drive, Zoey adjusted her bike helmet. Her long ponytails hung beneath her helmet as they rode their bikes lightning fast through the neighborhood.

Jasmine told Zoey, "Your friend Tommi seems nice. I knew it was just going to be a matter of time before you met some good people."

"Yeah, she is really nice, and she's in the Science Club too," Zoey said with a big smile, finally starting to feel like her new school might not be so bad after all.

"Well, I can't wait to meet her, Zoey."

"How much farther is Aubrey's house?" Zoey asked.

"There is her house," Jasmine said as she pointed to the large yellow-and-white stucco home with the girl standing in front of it waving frantically, three houses down from where they were. Jasmine and Zoey rode up the driveway and got off their bikes. Immediately, Aubrey ran up to Jasmine as if she hadn't seen her in over a month. Jasmine introduced Zoey, and then Aubrey introduced the girls to her older brother Noah and his friend Trevor, who were both sweaty from playing basketball in the driveway.

Aubrey said, "Let's hang out in the backyard by the pool."

Jasmine and Zoey followed her. Jasmine hadn't known that Aubrey had a brother and was a little caught off guard with the way he seemed to look at her. Both boys were tall, but Noah was a lot taller than his friend Trevor and couldn't seem to take his eyes off Jasmine. Jasmine took one last look at Noah and found him staring at her.

Just then Trevor yelled, "Yo! Are we gonna play ball or what, Noah?"

Aubrey said, "C'mon, slowpoke," and Jasmine followed her to the pool.

"I didn't know that you had an older brother," Jasmine said to Aubrey.

Taking a seat by the pool, Aubrey said casually, "Yeah, he goes to our school. He's in the eighth grade."

Aubrey asked Zoey who her teacher was at Briar Ridge.

Zoey said, "Mrs. Pennington."

"Oh, Mrs. P. She was one of my favorite teachers," she said fondly.

The girls laughed and talked as they sat poolside with their feet splashing in the water, and before they knew it, it was almost seven o'clock. Jasmine and Zoey said goodbye to Aubrey and her parents before they got on their bikes to go back home.

Riding their bikes through the neighborhood toward home, Zoey said, "And don't think for a moment that I didn't see you staring at her brother." Both girls busted out laughing.

"Besides, I wasn't the one staring." Jasmine told her. "But you gotta admit that he was cute."

"Yeah, he was," Zoey said as they peddled their way back to Wrenwood Drive.

When they got home, their dad was just putting the lawnmower away and looked up and said, "Perfect timing, girls. How was your friend's house?"

"It was fine. She has a pool!" Jasmine said excitedly. "We had a good time, and she lives really close."

"Glad you girls had a good time! Now go on inside and I will be in soon."

Zoey had already started to research the materials that she would need for her Ohm's law science project. She decided to go downstairs to talk to her dad about her supply list. He was in the family room stretched out on the worn leather sofa, watching the news. Zoey noticed that he had fallen asleep watching TV again. Although this was pretty usual for him, her dad never liked to admit that he was actually asleep. He would only admit to resting his eyes.

Tapping him lightly on his shoulder, Zoey said, "Dad ... wake up."

Stirring and clearing his throat, he replied, "I wasn't asleep. What do you need, baby girl?"

"Daddy, I wanted to show you my supply list of materials that I need for my science fair project."

As her dad sat up on the couch, he took the list that she made and read through it. "Looks like you're on top of your project, Zoe. How about we go out this weekend to pick up your supplies? I can think of a couple of items that you left off, but you did a real good job with making your list. I'm real proud of you, baby girl!" he said affectionately and gave her a high five.

Zoey felt very proud. "Thank you, Daddy. Now I think you should go to bed before you fall back asleep," she said as she went up to get ready for bed.

He yelled back, "I wasn't asleep!" as he stretched back out on the couch to finish watching the news.

Mrs. P. stood at the door of the classroom and greeted all her students as they walked in. Zoey noticed that today she was wearing a bright-pink shirt with a big puffy bow that tied at the side of her neck and a navy-blue skirt. Zoey wondered if Mrs. P. had gotten dressed in the dark this morning, because she wasn't her usual fashionable self.

"Good morning, Zoey."

"Good morning, Mrs. P."

Zoey walked in, said hello to Tommi and Josh Hightower, and quickly found her seat. Once everyone was seated, Mrs. P. got started on the lessons for the day. There was a pop quiz in math, and once they were done, Mrs. P. told everyone to switch papers with their neighbor. Zoey had to exchange papers with Jackson Smith, and she was not happy about it. Zoey thought, *I will have to keep an eye on him to make sure that he doesn't stick his pencil up his nose, because I don't want any little boogies on my paper!*

Mrs. P. went through the answers pretty quickly. By the time she reviewed question number six, Jackson hadn't made a move to put his pencil up his nose yet. Zoey was hopeful and thought, *Maybe he won't do it.* Mrs. P. reviewed question number nine ... then number ten! Zoey felt so relieved and then noticed that before he marked her grade, he did it again! In utter disgust, she looked over at Jackson Smith, and he had the audacity to look over and smile.

"You only missed one," he said. "How many did I miss?"

Still staring in disgust, she found her words and told him, "You didn't miss any."

He gave her a big goofy-looking grin, and it looked like he puffed up his chest as he said, "I'd be happy to help you study, Zoey."

Zoey wasn't sure why he was looking at her and smiling in such a goofy way, but she wanted to respond as nicely as possible.

"No, Jackson. I'll be fine, but thank you for the offer."

She took her paper back and gave it a quick once-over to make sure there were no boogies on it.

Mrs. P. told them all to put their papers away and to get ready for lunch.

As the students entered the cafeteria, the packers went to find seats first. Tommi packed her lunch also, so she and Zoey found seats and started talking about their science projects.

Zoey said, "My dad said that we will go out this weekend to get my supplies for my project."

"Oh good! My dad said he will take me out this weekend too."

"I can't wait to get started," Zoey said, eating her pretzels.

Just then two girls walked up and sat down. They were both smiling and had just gone through the lunch line. "Hey, Olivia and Emily. This is Zoey," said Tommi.

"Hi," said Zoey.

Tommi said, "Zoey is the new girl."

The girls replied in unison, "We know!"

Emily said, "Tommi was the new girl last year."

Zoey thought that pink must be Emily's favorite color because everything she had on was bright pink—even her shoes.

"I heard," Zoey said. "You all seem like you have been here forever."

They chuckled and talked as they ate the school pizza. Emily said, "Me and Olivia have gone here since kindergarten, but I only just met Tommi this summer at Girl Scout camp."

"Girl Scout camp? I thought that Girl Scouts only sold cookies," Zoey said.

Emily laughed and then said rather dramatically, "We do a lot more than just sell cookies! We are explorers discovering our superpowers, and we get to have fun at summer camp. This summer we climbed a rock-climbing wall and got to go horseback riding while we were at camp."

Tommi said, "Yeah. This was my first summer at camp, and it was a lot of fun."

Then Olivia said, "And I met Tommi last year when they moved into the house next door to mine, and now we're all good friends!"

"Hey, Zoey, did you bring your hot sauce today?" Tommi asked.

Zoey reached in her bag and gave the bottle to Tommi.

Olivia scrunched up her face and said, "Who brings hot sauce to school?" She started to laugh mockingly.

Zoey looked at her a bit miffed and said, "I do! What's wrong with that?"

Tommi quickly said, "What's so funny? I wish the school would have hot sauce instead of only ketchup. I like hot sauce."

Emily said, "I like hot sauce too!"

Olivia let out a nervous laugh and said, "Oh no ... there's nothing wrong with it. I've just never seen anyone bring their own bottle to school before."

Zoey had had just about enough of Olivia's snide comments and said, "I don't really care about what other kids do. I pack hot sauce in my bag because I like it, and it's the only way that I will eat my turkey sandwiches."

Olivia regretted having made the comment and gave an apologetic smile to Zoe.

Tommi changed the subject. "Zoey, are you going to the Harvest Fest this weekend?"

"I don't know. I've seen the signs up around the school and community. What is it?"

"It's a lot of fun for the entire family. They usually have rides and games and a few bands that play," said Olivia.

Tommi said, "You should come! It's a lot of fun, and everyone will be there!"

"Okay, cool! I'll ask my mom when I get home and let you know later tonight. Remember to give me your phone number before school lets out."

Mrs. P. was standing at the door of the cafeteria with her big puffy pink bow, which meant lunchtime was over. The girls quickly cleaned up their area and went to get in line to walk back to class.

Chapter 4

Harvest Festival

Thankfully, that afternoon flew by, and Mrs. P. didn't give another pop quiz or test, or any homework, since it was the weekend. She told her students to have a great weekend and that she might see some of them at the Harvest Fest. Her students tidied up their desks and quickly packed up to go home. Tommi had written down her number on a scrap piece of paper and handed it to Zoey on their way out the door.

When Zoey got home, she dropped her backpack in the corner of the hallway and headed into the kitchen to get her after-school snack. Jasmine was already home and leaning on the kitchen counter eating some watermelon that their mom had cut up the day before.

"Zoe, take your backpack to your room, please," said her mom as she headed outside to check the mailbox.

"Sure thing, Mom, but can I take it up after my snack?"

Her mom turned and looked at her. Zoey quickly went to pick up her backpack and took it upstairs. When she came back down to get a bowl of cut-up watermelon, Jasmine was still leaning on the kitchen counter.

"Mom gave you her 'don't you try me today' look," she said teasingly to Zoey.

"Yeah, I know ... Mom meant business!" They sat in the kitchen and talked about their day, and Zoey asked her if she heard about the Harvest Festival.

"Aubrey and some of the other kids at school were telling me about it. It sounds like a lot of fun."

"I know," said Zoey. "Do you think you might want to go?"

"Want to go where?" asked Mom as she dropped the mail on the kitchen counter.

"To the Harvest Festival that is happening this weekend," Jasmine told her. "It's held at the Briar Township Community Center, and they have food, music, and games, and supposedly everyone goes."

"Oh yeah. One of our neighbors was telling me about it. It lasts the entire weekend," her mom said as she looked through the drawer for the Antonio's Pizza carryout menu. "Sounds like a lot of fun! If you girls want to go, we can go tomorrow. It will be a good way to get out and meet some of our neighbors. We'll make it a family outing."

Friday nights were a lot of fun in the Lyndon household. Every Friday was Pizza Night, usually with a movie or a game. Tonight was Jasmine's night to pick the game, and she chose Uno. Dad got home and had stopped and picked up the pizzas from Antonio's Pizza. Mom had pulled out the paper plates and napkins, because no one liked to clean up on Fridays.

After playing a couple rounds of Uno, Zoey blurted out, "Hey, wait a minute! Daddy ... where did all your cards go?"

She held up the game to do a quick check to see where her dad might have hidden his cards.

"David, are you over there cheating again?" Mom asked with her patented raised eyebrow and pursed lips.

Jasmine pulled out four cards from under the leather sofa cushion and glared at her dad in disbelief.

Their dad busted out laughing. "I'm sorry ... but I was not about to get stuck with all those cards," he replied, still laughing. "I had two reverse cards, a green zero, and a red five."

"David, you are setting a terrible example for the girls. You should be ashamed of yourself," Mom said, trying not to laugh at her husband.

"Girls, I'm sorry! Mom is right. I wasn't setting the best example for the two of you. I think we should call it a wrap."

Everyone agreed, and Jasmine collected the Uno cards and put them back in the box. When her dad stood up to head upstairs, six more cards fell onto the floor.

"Daddy!" the girls called out in unison with their mouths left open in shock.

Laughing again, he threw his hands up to claim his innocence. "What?" He started walking toward the steps.

"C'mon, you big cheater," Mom said as she pushed him out of the family room. "Girls, we are going to go watch a movie upstairs," she told them as she picked up the last of the pizza boxes and paper plates.

"Okay, Mom. Me and Zoey will stay down here and watch some movies."

Zoey stretched out on the sofa while Jasmine sat at the opposite end of the sofa with her ankles crossed on the coffee table. The girls watched a movie and talked about how they liked their new schools.

"So, I take it that things are going pretty well for you at school?" Jasmine asked.

"Yeah it is, especially since I've made some friends and joined the Science Club. Plus, I really like Mrs. P.," Zoey told her as they watched *Pretty Woman* for the umpteenth time. "How do you like your school?" Zoey asked.

"I think this might be a pretty good year. I've noticed a couple of really cute boys, and Aubrey is a lot of fun. She's in most of my classes."

ZOEY LYNDON'S BIG MOVE TO THE LOU

"Does Aubrey's brother go to your school?"

Jasmine tried to hide her smile. "Yes, Noah goes to my school."

In a teasing tone, Zoey asked, "So when did we get on a first-name basis with Mr. Noah?"

Nudging Zoey's feet with her thigh, Jasmine said, "Stop being silly, Zoe."

"Okay, okay, I promise. I'm just glad that you like your new school too."

"Me too, Zoe."

"Tommi told me today that her parents are divorced."

"A lot of kids' parents are divorced, Zoe. That's kind of normal."

"Well, I hope not! I don't want Mom and Dad to get a divorce."

"We don't have to worry about that happening. Mom and Dad are crazy about each other! You see the two of them always playing kissy face?"

"Yeah, I do. That is so gross, though!"

Jasmine decided to change the subject. "Do you need any help picking out something to wear for tomorrow?"

"No, I don't think so. I think I'm going to wear my new floral bibs."

"Ooh yeah, that'll be cute," said Jasmine.

The girls stayed up just watching movies and being silly. Finally, their dad told them it was getting pretty late. They both knew that what he really meant was that it was time for bed.

"Night, Daddy," Zoey said to her father as she walked upstairs to get ready for bed.

"Good night, baby girl."

Jasmine stayed behind talking to her dad as he turned off all the lights and set the security alarm.

The sweet smell of funnel cake, cotton candy, popcorn, and caramel apples filled the air as the Lyndon family tried to take in all the attractions of the Harvest Festival. There was a local band singing "Don't You Wish Your Girlfriend Was Hot like Me" by the Pussycat Dolls, and Zoey thought they sounded pretty good. There was a haunted house that seemed to be pretty interesting, a Ferris wheel, and a large carousel.

Jasmine was scoping the crowd for her friend Aubrey and spotted her at the hotdog stand.

She asked, "Mom and Dad, do you mind if I walk around with my friends?"

"I don't have a problem with that," her father said, looking at his wife to see if she was okay with it.

"It's fine with me. Let's agree to meet at the carousel in an hour and a half," her mom told her.

"Thanks, Mom. I'll see you guys in ninety minutes," Jasmine said before running off to hang out with her friends.

"Hey, Zoe, are any of your friends here?" asked her mom.

"Tommi said she is going to be here, but I haven't seen her yet."

"Well, how about we buy a few tickets so we can ride some of the rides," Dad asked.

"Sounds good to me," Mom said.

Zoey couldn't believe how crowded the Harvest Festival was and how many kids she saw from school. She was starting to wonder how much longer Tommi was going to be, because she didn't want to hang out with her mom and dad the entire time.

"Zoey, who is this?" her mom asked as she saw a small group of kids approaching.

Zoey turned around quickly to see if it was Tommi, but it wasn't. "Oh, these are some of my friends from school." It was Emily, Olivia, and Josh Hightower.

Zoey noticed that Emily was wearing her signature pink and sparkly. Today it was her glittery sneakers and pink sparkly jacket.

Emily said excitedly, "Hey, Zoey, glad you made it!"

"Hey Emily, Olivia, Josh! This is my mom and dad."

Her friends all smiled and said hello to her parents, and Zoey's parents responded in unison.

Emily asked Zoey if she wanted to ride the Ferris wheel. Zoey looked at her parents to see if it was okay, and they told her yes. Her mother told her to meet them at the carousel in half an hour. Zoey agreed and was off!

Zoey asked, "Has anyone seen Tommi? I was supposed to meet her here a while ago."

"Oh, she's not coming!" Olivia told her. "She was supposed to ride with us, but her mother said she got sick and had to stay home."

Zoey remembered that Olivia and Tommi lived next door to each other. "Oh, I hope she's okay," Zoey said. "I'll give her a call tomorrow to see how she's doing."

Josh asked, "Who wants to go to the haunted house?"

The girls all scrunched up their faces and quickly shook their heads no.

"Looks like it's three against one Josh," Olivia happily stated.

"Okay, okay, how about we use our tickets on some of the rides?" Josh asked.

The girls were all in agreement. They rode the gravity wheel once, and Emily's stomach felt a little queasy afterward. They also rode the Ferris wheel twice and stopped to get some cotton candy with the last of their tickets. Zoey looked at the time and realized that it was time for her to get back to her parents. She told her friends that she had to go and that she would see them at school.

As Zoey walked back to the carousel, she thought that Saint Louis might not be such a bad place after all. She had met some good friends and was really starting to enjoy living in Missouri. She was sorry to hear that Tommi was not feeling well and couldn't make it to the Harvest Festival.

She waved at her parents, who were already waiting for her at the carousel.

"Did you have a good time with your friends?" Her dad asked, throwing a handful of kettle corn into his mouth.

Smiling, Zoey said, "Yes! I'm so glad we came. I had so much fun!" She shook her head in amusement and teased, "Daddy, I think you're supposed to eat the popcorn and not waste it down your shirt."

Laughing and nodding his head in agreement, he replied, "I know, baby girl." He quickly tossed another handful of the sweet kettle corn into his mouth.

"Hey, Rachel, didn't Jasmine leave with her friend Aubrey?" Zoey's father asked his wife as he noticed a strange boy almost as tall as him walking with his daughter.

With her patented raised left eyebrow, her mom said "Um hmm..." as she also looked at the boy who was walking with Jasmine.

Smiling with a huge Cheshire grin across her face, Zoey thought that this was going to be good.

"Oh, that's just Noah," Zoey stated casually.

Her dad looked at her and wondered, *Who in the Sam Hill is Noah?*

"Hey, Daddy!" Jasmine beamed as she and Noah reached the carousel to meet her family. "This is Noah, Aubrey's brother."

"What happened to Aubrey?" her father asked suspiciously.

Looking at her husband in disbelief and in a stern voice usually reserved for the girls, Jasmine's mother said, "David!" Changing her tone just as quickly to her sweet-as-pie voice, she greeted Jasmine's friend. "Hello, Noah. How are you?"

"Hello, Mr. and Mrs. Lyndon," Noah nervously replied.

"Did you go to the haunted house?" Zoey blurted out as she took a look at the good-looking Noah. She thought that he was much cuter than she remembered.

Jasmine said, "Yes, and it was pretty scary." But her eyes never seemed to leave Noah's.

Having had just about enough of Jasmine's young friend, her father abruptly said "Thank you for escorting our daughter safely to us" as he reached out to shake Noah's hand.

Jasmine and Zoey waved goodbye to Noah as they headed back to their car to go home.

"So, did everyone have a good time?" Mom asked lightly.

"Oh my God! Mom, this was so much fun. I saw so many kids from school and even saw a couple of my teachers," Zoey said.

"What about you, Jasmine?" Mom asked.

"I had a good time! Aubrey is a lot of fun, and I liked listening to the band," she said, looking out the window as her father drove home.

Jasmine was just about to put her earbuds in her ears and listen to some music when her mom said, "So, tell me about Noah."

"What do you want to know?"

With pursed lips and her patented raised left eyebrow, her mother stated matter-of-factly, "You left with Aubrey and returned with Noah. How did you end up with Noah?"

"Well, Aubrey and I hung out for the entire time. We rode one of the rides, but mostly hung out in the pit and listened to the band. Right before I was going to walk back to meet you, Noah asked us if we had gone through the haunted house. We all

ZOEY LYNDON'S BIG MOVE TO THE LOU

went through the haunted house, and he asked me if he could walk me back to the carousel."

Zoey quickly chimed in telling her parents that Tommi was sick and that was why she hadn't shown up. She was really just trying to get the conversation onto something else because she knew that Jasmine didn't like being in the hot seat.

Jasmine silently mouthed the words "thank you" to Zoey as she put in her earbuds and turned up her music for the rest of the drive home.

Zoey called Tommi once they got home to see how she was feeling and to let her know how the Harvest Festival was. Tommi told her that she really wasn't sick, that she had started her period, and she just wanted to stay home. Zoey was glad to hear that she wasn't sick, and Tommi asked her to come over the next day. Zoey told her she would ask her parents and to keep her fingers crossed.

Zoey found her mom and dad in the kitchen eating ice cream. Dad was eating his favorite, butter pecan, and Mom was eating her favorite, mint chocolate chip.

"Can I go over to Tommi's house tomorrow?" she asked.

"Didn't you say she was sick?" her mom asked before taking a bite of her mint chocolate chip ice cream.

"She told me that she wasn't really sick and that she feels much better now," Zoey said.

Her dad and mom looked skeptical, and then her mom told her, "I don't think that's a good idea, Zoey. We don't need you going over there and getting sick."

Sighing heavily, Zoey leaned over and whispered in her mother's ear to let her know that Tommi had got her period and wasn't really sick.

"Oh, well, in that case, I don't have a problem with you going over to see your friend tomorrow," her mother said.

Zoey's dad gave her mom a questioning look but didn't say anything. Her mom responded to his look and said, "It's a girl thing," and that settled it.

"Thanks, Mom!" Zoey said as she smiled and gave her mom quick hug around her neck.

Zoey headed upstairs to Jasmine's room to see if she could find out more about Noah.

"Hey, sis!" Zoey said as she knocked on Jasmine's bedroom door and opened it simultaneously.

Jasmine grumbled, "I didn't tell you that you could come in."

"I'm sorry. I was just going to tell you that I'm going over to Tommi's house tomorrow."

"Did you already ask Mom and Dad?" Jasmine asked.

"Yep! What are you doing?" Zoey could clearly see that she was reading a book, but she asked the question anyway.

Placing her bookmark in her book, she closed it and put it next to her on the bed. Jasmine replied, "I was trying to read! What do you want?"

Zoey plopped down on the bottom of Jasmine's bed and leaned in with a wicked little grin and told her, "I want the 411."

Smiling and shaking her head in disbelief at how nosy her little sister was, she said, "There's nothing to tell."

"Nothing to tell my foot! How did you and Noah end up walking back together today?" Zoey asked.

"Well, Miss Nosy Pants, I told you already that Aubrey and I hung out a little bit. Before I was going to head back to meet Mom and Dad, Noah asked if we had gone through the haunted house yet. You know I don't like scary stuff, so I wasn't planning on doing the haunted house. Then Noah and his friends asked if we had gone through it and we said no, and he grabbed Aubrey's hand, and we went."

"So how did he end up walking you back?" Zoey asked.

"Well, it's kind of embarrassing, but when we were in the haunted house, this man jumped out at me and scared me so bad, I thought I was going to pee on myself. I jumped and screamed, and Noah was behind me. He put his hand on my shoulder and asked me if I was okay. I tried to keep my cool and said yes, but I don't think he believed me."

Zoey asked her, "Why don't you think he believed you?"

"Because after that he said that there were some other scary parts and asked if I wanted him to hold my hand. So I said yes!"

"Wow!" Zoey's face was lit up like a Christmas tree. She had never even thought about holding a boy's hand before, and this information was a lot juicier than she had imagined.

She asked her sister, "So how was it?"

"How was what?"

"Did it feel weird holding his hand?"

Jasmine told her, "No silly, it didn't feel weird, and I am not talking about this anymore with you."

"Okay, okay. I won't ask any more questions," Zoey said. She was still trying to process all the juicy info she had just gotten from her sister. The most interesting things that usually happened in her fourth-grade world were finding out which new boy Olivia liked this week or watching Jackson Smith stick pencils up his nose during class.

Changing the subject, Jasmine asked, "So I take it that Tommi is feeling better?"

"She told me that she really wasn't sick, but that she got her period and wanted to stay home," Zoey told her.

"Oh! I know that was a bummer for her!" Jasmine said with an understanding look. "That is not something anyone is ever ready for, but I'm sure she'll be all right!"

Zoey knew that Jasmine had got her period earlier this year, and their mom had had "the talk" with both girls a couple of times already. Although Zoey had not gotten her period yet, she knew it would be coming soon enough.

"Zoey, I'd like to get back to my book now," Jasmine said.

"Okay, okay. I was about to go get ready for bed anyway," Zoey said as she got up from her sister's bed and walked out of her room.

"Close my door!" Jasmine yelled to Zoey as she opened her book and removed the book-mark to continue reading.

Chapter 5
Finding Her Way

In the Lyndon household, Sunday mornings were reserved for church and usually a good home-cooked meal. Sundays were spent relaxing around the house and finishing up any homework that was given over the weekend.

"Zoey, you need to make sure that all your homework is done before you go over to your friend's house," her mother told her.

"Okay, Mom, I only had one worksheet to complete for math class, and that shouldn't take me that long to knock out." Zoey grabbed a handful of grapes from the refrigerator and headed upstairs to tackle her homework.

"I thought you were going over to your friend's house," Jasmine said as she was on her way into the kitchen to see what Mom was cooking for dinner.

"Mom said I have to do my homework first," Zoey said as she continued to her room.

After Zoey finished her homework, her mom dropped her off at Tommi's house. Ms. Mitchell was standing outside talking to a neighbor when they pulled up, so Zoey's mom went over to introduce herself.

"Hello, I'm Rachel Lyndon, Zoey's mother," she said, reaching to shake her hand.

"Hi, Rachel. It's nice to meet you. I'm Tonya Mitchell, Tomasina's mother," she said with a friendly smile.

"It is nice to finally meet you. My daughter talks about Tommi all the time."

"Oh trust me, I understand. I've been hearing about Miss Zoey Lyndon nonstop since the beginning of school," Tonya said with a chuckle.

"What time would you like for me to pick her up?" Rachel asked.

"You don't need to pick her up if you don't want to, because I have to go to the grocery store later today. I can drop her off when I'm on my way to the store in about two hours, if that's okay with you," Tonya said.

"Sure, that works for me." She gave Zoey a quick hug, told her to mind her manners, and then left.

Tommi grabbed Zoey by her right hand and pulled her into the house and up the stairs to her bedroom. "Geez ... I thought your mom would never leave!" she said with an exasperated look.

Zoey laughed "I know. I was thinking the same thing."

Tommi closed her bedroom door and plopped down crisscross style on her bed and said, "Okay, tell me everything! What did I miss yesterday?"

Zoey laughed at her friend's silliness and eagerly filled her in on the events from the last twenty-four hours.

"So, I really liked the Harvest Festival and couldn't believe how many people were there from school."

"Yeah, Yeah, I know. Everyone always goes every year," Tommi said.

"Well, a lot of people asked about you and were surprised that you weren't there yesterday.

Olivia just told everyone you were sick, and everyone felt sorry that you had to miss it."

Tommi gave a lopsided grin and motioned for Zoey to continue.

"Emily, Olivia, and Josh Hightower all came to find me yesterday, and we all hung out. We hung around the pit for a little bit and listened to the band. They were really good! We ate cotton candy, and then we split funnel cake."

Throwing her hands in the air in exasperation, Tommi interrupted Zoey. "Aw, man! I can't believe I missed the funnel cake. Their funnel cakes are huge," she said with a pouty face.

"I know," said Zoey with a teasing smile.

Rolling her eyes, Tommi asked, "What else did you guys do?"

"We rode some of the rides, and every ride that we rode, Olivia just had to sit with Josh Hightower."

Tommi giggled at Zoey's comment and replied, "Yeah, Olivia is kind of boy crazy, in case you haven't noticed."

"I thought she liked the boy who sits at the table next to ours in the cafeteria," Zoey said with a puzzled look on her face. She started to connect the dots. It was as if Tommi could see her brain working, and then both girls just started laughing.

Deciding to turn the conversation in another direction, Zoey said, "I hope you don't think I'm being too nosy, but what is it like?" She had a serious look on her face.

Tommi paused and then realized what she was asking. "It's terrible! And I absolutely hate it!"

"Had you and your mom talked about it before?"

"Yeah, we did, but I never thought it would happen while I was in the fourth grade, Zoey. I thought it would happen, like, a long time from now ... like when I was in the sixth grade or something. I told my mom that I'm probably the only girl in the entire fourth grade that got her stupid period!"

Zoey wanted to try to make her friend feel better and told her that she was sure that there were other girls in the school who had started their period.

Giving her a skeptical look, Tommi asked, "Have you got your period yet?"

Zoey shook her head no. "Not yet, but my sister has, and she told me that it wasn't bad ... just annoying sometimes."

"Luckily, it only comes once a month. And now you need to hurry up and get yours so that I'm not alone," Tommi said, giving a gentle nudge to her friend.

Both girls giggled, and although Zoey knew that she would have to deal with it at some point, she secretly hoped it would not come until she was in middle school.

Zoey asked Tommi how she was coming with her edible DNA science project. Tommi told her and then got up to play some music on her vintage record player.

"Oh my God! That is so cool, Tommi, You have your own stereo!" Zoey said, walking over to get a closer look.

Laughing, she said, "No, silly. It's not a stereo; it's a record player. My dad got it for me for my birthday this year. He always says that music sounds the best when it's played on vinyl."

Still in awe of the record player, Zoey asked, "What's vinyl?"

Tommi took the record out of Michael Jackson's *Thriller* album and held it up. "This is vinyl," she said before playing her favorite song. "Zoey, do you like Michael Jackson?"

"Yes, of course." She thought, *Who doesn't like Michael Jackson?*

They listened to "P.Y.T.," Tommi's favorite song, three times, as well as several other songs while Tommi showed Zoey the progress she had made on her science project. Zoey was impressed and asked if she had any help. Tommi told her that her dad had helped her label her different chemical bases, and she used toothpicks to connect the chemical bases to make them look like ladders, which took forever.

"It looks great, Tommi!"

"Thanks, Zoe. Let's go outside and play before my mom has to take you home," Tommi said as she turned off her record player and put the record back in the sleeve.

Tommi picked up a bright-blue piece of sidewalk chalk and drew a big hopscotch board so they could play. They took turns, and when Zoey had rolled her rock on the number 6, Tommi's mom came out and said it was time to go. The girls persuaded her to allow them to each have one more turn before they drove Zoey home.

Chapter 6

Science Project

Over the next couple of weeks, Zoey worked diligently on her science project. After getting home from school, she would quickly finish her chores and her homework so she could work on her project. She chose Ohm's law for her science fair project. Zoey discovered that Ohm's law was a basic equation: voltage = current x resistance, or $V = I \times R$.

She learned during her research that voltage is the source of energy, and the current is the flow of charge. Electrical power in a circuit is the rate that energy is absorbed or produced within that circuit. Power can be used for light bulbs or heaters.

Zoey was pleased with her project and the way that it had come together. As she put the finishing touches on the trifold board (a standard at every science fair), she thought that everything looked good.

"It looks good, baby girl," her father said as he stood in the entrance to the kitchen.

"Oh, hey, Dad. I didn't see you standing there," she said.

"Do you need any help with anything?"

"No. I just finished up my trifold board, and I think I'm ready," she said.

"Do you need anything else for your presentation?" he asked.

"No, Daddy. I think I'm good."

"Looks like you're ready to me. When is the big day again?"

Zoey smiled proudly and told him, "It's the day after tomorrow. I can't wait to see Tommi's edible DNA project and Josh Hightower's growing crystals. Tommi showed me her project before she completed it, and it looked pretty awesome."

Hmm ... the growing crystals sound interesting, her father thought. "Why don't you clean off the table and go ahead and get yourself ready for bed. It's already past your bedtime."

"Okay, Daddy," she said.

He winked at her before heading into the family room to watch the news with her mom. Zoey finished cleaning up and took one last look at her project before turning off the lights and heading upstairs to get ready for bed. She smiled to herself and thought her project looked pretty awesome and couldn't wait for her friends to see it. She got ready for bed and looked forward to tomorrow.

"Zoey, you're going to need your raincoat this morning. It's raining cats and dogs out there!"

"Ugh! I hate when it rains," Zoey told her mom as she rolled her eyes and put on her bright-yellow raincoat.

Zoey finished the last of her orange juice before placing her cup in the sink. She picked up her neon-orange backpack, which she was glad was water resistant, and headed off to school.

"Do you want to wait until the rain slows down a bit before you get out?" her mom asked as she pulled her big blue jeep up in front of Briar Ridge to drop her off.

"No, I don't want to be late." Zoey grabbed her backpack and umbrella before stepping out of the car. "I hope I don't drown in this monsoon!" she said before closing the car door and running into the building.

Mrs. P. was standing at the classroom door passing out plastic bags for everyone to put their umbrellas in to try to keep the floor from getting soaking wet. Zoey really liked her navy-blue, green, and red wide-leg plaid overalls. They had eight buttons down the front, and she had on a navy-blue turtleneck. Zoey thought that Mrs. P. had great style!

"Good morning, class. I'm glad to see the rain didn't delay any of you this morning," Mrs. P. said as she finished wiping up the wet floor to prevent anyone from slipping. "Let me say that I am extremely proud of all of you who have decided to participate in the Briar Ridge

Science Fair this year. I know that several of you will not be able to attend the event tomorrow evening, so I would like for those students who are participating to please briefly describe your project to the class. I will give you each five minutes and another two minutes for questions."

She was greeted with smiles and excitement from the entire class. Zoey thought this was a great idea and couldn't wait to hear about everyone's projects. The classroom grew louder because of the buzz of expectation, so Mrs. P. had to quickly restore the order back to her class.

"But first, please take out your spelling books and turn to page sixty-two so that we can review before your test this week."

She was met with load groans and mumbling from her students, to which she couldn't hide her smile. "I know, I know ... but the sooner we get done with our review, the quicker we can hear from our science fair participants."

They spent the next fifty minutes reviewing the spelling lesson, and Mrs. P. went over the weekly announcements. She had the students exchange their social studies homework from over the weekend, and they graded one another's homework assignments.

"I am so excited that we have almost half of our class participating in this year's science fair! We have eight students participating. I have never had that many of my students participating in the science fair, and I am so very proud of all their hard work! Josh, are you ready?"

Trying not to smile, he said, "Yes, Mrs. P." He quickly walked to the front of the classroom to talk about his project. "I chose to do my project on growing crystals. There are several types of growing crystals that you can do, but I chose to do the rock candy growing crystals. The supplies that I needed were pretty basic. I used sugar, water, a pan, a small plate, a glass, a spoon, wax paper, several glass jars, food coloring, and wooden skewers. A crystal is a solid material with atoms and molecules that form in a repeating pattern. This rock candy project allowed me to mimic the repeating pattern that crystals make. I did a couple of experimental batches before completing my project. Once I completed the process, I started to see crystals form within a couple of days, and within a couple of weeks, the crystals were formed into a nice cluster on the skewer sticks. This project was a lot of fun, and I was able to complete most of it on my own. I only needed help when I had to boil the water-and-sugar solution."

"This is what Josh's rock candy crystals look like," Mrs. P. said as she stood at the front of the class holding up a picture of rock candy crystals from one of her books. "Does anyone have any questions for Josh?"

A few students raised their hands to ask questions, but because of the time limit, Josh only had time to answer two. Everyone gave him a round of applause as Josh returned to his seat.

"Tomasina, would you like to go next?" Mrs. P. asked.

"I'm ready," Tommi said as she looked over at Zoey with a nervous smile.

Zoey smiled back, giving her a big thumbs up.

"My science fair project was edible DNA. DNA is the distinctive characteristics that every living thing has. Its genetic code determines the characteristics of each of us. DNA stands for deoxyribonucleic acid. Our bodies have tons of cells, and these cells contain molecules called DNA. The DNA molecule looks like a twisted ladder and is called a helix. I chose this project because I thought it would be informative and fun. My supplies were Twizzlers, different-color gumdrops, toothpicks, and cups. I sorted out the different-color gumdrops into four different cups and labeled each cup. There are four nucleotides: adenine, thymine, cytosine, and guanine. Nucleotides are molecules are the basic building blocks of DNA. Adernine and thymine are always paired together, and cytosine and guanine are always paired together. Assembling my edible DNA project only took me a couple of days once I had everything sorted out."

"Good job, Tomasina! Would anyone like to ask Tomasina a question about her project?"

"I have a question, Mrs. P.," Jackson Smith said as he raised his hand. "Tommi, will you bring your edible DNA project to class so that we can taste it after the science fair is over?"

Some of the kids laughed at his question, while others were in agreement with him.

"Jackson, no one will want to actually eat these projects because of how many times the candies have been touched by Tomasina's hands and the judges' hands," Mrs. P. told him.

Jackson mumbled under his breath, "I'll still eat it!"

No one else got to ask Tommi any questions, and Mrs. P. had two other students talk about their projects. After that it was time for lunch.

"Since we didn't have enough time to hear from everyone before lunch, we will get the remaining four students after lunch. Packers, please grab your lunch, and everyone let's line up for lunch."

"Hey, save us a seat!" Emily called out to Zoey as they made their way through the lunch line.

"No problem," Zoey said as she headed to Mrs. P.'s tables with the rest of the packers. She pulled out her hand sanitizer, which was clipped to the handle of her lunch box, and gave a couple of quick squeezes to her palm. After rubbing her hands together to make sure her hands were clean, she clipped the hand sanitizer back to her lunch box. Zoey pulled out her turkey sandwich and her small bottle of hot sauce and put several drops on her sandwich. She slid the bottle back into her lunch box and began to eat her lunch as she waited for her friends to work their way through the dreaded cafeteria line.

"Ooh, I love pizza day," Tommi said as she sat down across from Zoey. Emily and Olivia were right behind Tommi, and Emily took the seat next to Zoey while Olivia sat across from Emily and next to Tommi.

"Good job, Tommi, on talking about your science fair project," Zoey said.

"Yeah, Tommi. I can't wait to see your edible DNA project tomorrow," Olivia told her.

Emily said, "Yeah, both your and Josh Hightower's projects seem really interesting."

"Thanks, guys!" Tommi beamed. "I'll be glad when tomorrow is over, I'm starting to get a little bit nervous about my presentation," she said as she took a bite of her pizza.

Nibbling on her pretzels, Zoey told her, "I know what you mean. At first I wasn't nervous, but the more time goes by, I'm starting to get a little nervous too."

"Excuse me, Zoey. Josh told me that you have hot sauce." Zoey looked up and saw Jackson. "Do you mind if I use some for my pizza? I like hot sauce on my pizza," he said.

"Sure, but bring it right back," Zoey said as she gave Jackson her hot sauce.

"No problem. Be right back," he said as he headed back to his seat.

"OMG ... he is so cute!" Olivia stated with a dreamy look in her eyes.

"Seriously, Olivia! He is so gross!" Tommi blurted out.

"I don't want to be mean, but yeah, he is kind of gross," Emily told her friend.

"I never said that he wasn't gross. I said he is cute!" Olivia said in exasperation with a huge sigh.

The girls all looked at each other and cracked up laughing.

"I don't really know him as well as you all do, but I guess I've never paid that much attention to him. I'll have to give him a good look to see how cute he really is," Zoey said.

As if on cue, Jackson brought back Zoey's bottle of hot sauce. "Thanks, Zoey."

The girls all busted out laughing and tried not to look at Jackson.

Jackson looked at them suspiciously and said, "I don't even want to know," and then he turned and walked back to his seat.

Finally, Zoey let go of her laughter after having to hold it while talking to Jackson.

"Okay, Okay, Olivia, I will give it to you on your call. Jackson is cute," Zoey reluctantly admitted.

"Yeah he is, but he is still gross," Tommi said.

When lunch was over, Mrs. P.'s class headed back to the classroom to work on the afternoon assignments. Normally they would be allowed to go outside, but because it was literally a monsoon outside, Mrs. P. gave the class fifteen minutes of free time. Some kids read a book at their desk, and others played video games. Zoey pulled out one of her Mackenzie Blue books to read.

The afternoon was spent delving into the wonderful world of fractions. Zoey wondered if anyone actually enjoyed fractions, and if so, she thought something must be wrong with them. Mrs. P. saved the remainder of the afternoon to allow for the students participating in the school science fair to talk about their projects.

Zoey was excited to talk about her Ohm's law project and knew this would help to calm her nerves for the next day. Jackson talked about his project, which was exploring the pH balance of soil. Someone else presented on Newton's law and exploring corrosion.

"Great job to all my science fair participants, and I can't wait to see everyone's completed work tomorrow. It looks like the rain has finally stopped, just in time for all of you to make it home. See you all tomorrow!" Mrs. P. told her class as she erased the chalkboard.

Once Zoey arrived home, she walked into the kitchen for her after-school snack and dropped her backpack in the hallway corner. "Hey, Jazz," she greeted her sister, who was already eating some of the cookies that her mom had baked last night.

"Hey, Zoe, there are still cookies left if you want some."

"Oh, cool," she said as she opened the cookie container on the counter. She took out three cookies. She got a small glass from the cabinet and poured herself some milk.

"I decided to try out for our school play, *The Sound of Music*," Jasmine said as she ate her last bite.

"Wow! That sounds exciting. You have a great voice. You should definitely get a good part. When are the auditions?"

"Thanks. The auditions are tomorrow, and Noah is going to try out too." She beamed.

"Noah! What about Aubrey?"

"Oh, Aubrey doesn't want to try out, and apparently Noah was the lead in last year's production of *The Hunchback of Notre Dame*."

"Um hmm!" Zoey said with her mother's patented raised eyebrow and smirk. "So is Noah your boyfriend now?" she asked.

Before Jasmine could answer, their mother stepped into the kitchen and told Zoey to take her backpack up to her room. Jasmine gave Zoey a wicked little smile realizing that she had been saved by the bell.

"Okay, Mom," Zoey said. And then she said to Jasmine, "I still want an answer to my question." She put her dirty glass and plate in the dishwasher and grabbed her backpack to take up to her room. Their mom told the girls to go ahead and tackle their homework while she cooked dinner.

"What's for dinner?" Jasmine asked.

"Meat loaf, mashed potatoes, and green beans."

"Sounds good to me." Jasmine loved her mother's meat loaf and gave her mom a thumbs-up before heading up to her room to knock out her homework.

Her mom chuckled and said, "Glad you approve."

When Zoey finished her homework, she knocked on Jasmine's door and asked if she could come in. Jasmine was still finishing up her homework. Zoey asked if she would listen to her while she went over her presentation for tomorrow's science fair.

"Sure. Give me about fifteen minutes to finish up," Jasmine told her.

"Great! Just come to my room when you're done."

Jasmine answered the last four questions on her math homework, and then she went to Zoey's rooms to hear her Ohm's law presentation.

Zoey had already opened her trifold poster board and had her experiment, which was housed in a recycled shoebox. She had placed a battery holder with metal clips and two wires with alligator clips connected to a tiny light bulb inside the shoebox. She tested the brightness of the light bulb based upon its contact with various metals. She further explained that voltage equals current multiplied by resistance.

"Wow! Zoey, that was great! You really did a good job with your presentation," Jasmine said with pride.

"Thanks." Zoey beamed. "I worked really hard on it."

"I can tell," Jasmine said as she stood up to leave and go back to her own room.

"And don't think that I forgot about my question earlier," Zoey said, catching her by surprise.

Trying to act like she didn't know what her little sister was talking about, Jasmine responded innocently, "What question?"

"The one about Noah being your boyfriend."

"Dang ... why are you always up in my business?" she said in exasperation as she leaned against the doorway.

"Why do you have to be so secretive?" Zoey asked as she cocked her head to the side and placed her hand on her imaginary hip.

"No, he is not my boyfriend! I like him, and he likes me. Okay, Miss Nosy Pants?"

Zoey looked at her suspiciously and said, "Okay, if you say so."

Jasmine shook her head and went back to her room.

"Girls, time for dinner!" their mother yelled up the stairs.

Over dinner the Lyndon family discussed their day while they enjoyed their savory meal.

"I've decided to try out for the school play tomorrow," Jasmine announced just before taking another bite of her mashed potatoes.

"Oh, that's great, honey! What is the play?" asked her mother.

"*The Sound of Music*," she answered.

"You have such a beautiful voice, Jazz; you're sure to get a good part," her father said. Winking at his wife, he said, "Rachel, you know you put your foot in this meatloaf!"

Nodding her head in agreement, she said, "Thank you, babe. I'm glad you like it."

The girls agreed that their mom's meatloaf was extra good tonight. Zoey asked her parents if they would be able to come to see her presentation tomorrow, since it was during the school day. They both assured her that they would not miss it for the world. They had seen all the hard work that she had put into her science project over the last several weeks. Jasmine told her that she hated that she would have to miss her presentation, but "I know you're going to blow it out of the water."

That night as Zoey got ready for bed, her father came in to tuck her in. Sitting at the foot of her bed, he asked, "So are you nervous about tomorrow's presentation, baby girl?"

Zoey said, "A little, Daddy" with a little smile.

Squeezing her leg, he encouraged her. "You'll do great, Zoe. I've got something for you that might help with your presentation." He handed her a laser pointer. "I use this at work sometimes during my presentations or if I am out in one of the manufacturing facilities and need to point to a specific piece of equipment."

Zoey sat up in the bed and took the laser pointer from her dad and started pointing to the ceiling so that she could see the little red dot light up. "This is so cool! Thanks, Daddy." She beamed, still playing with the laser pointer.

"Glad you like it." He smiled back at her and got up to give her a kiss good night. He told her to get some sleep and then headed over to Jasmine's room to tell her good night.

"Night, Daddy."

"Good night, baby girl."

Chapter 7

It's Showtime

The next morning when the girls came down-stairs for their usual bowl of cereal and toast, they were surprised to see a big breakfast and that their father was still home.

Taking a piece off the mound of bacon that her mother had cooked, Jasmine asked, "What is the special occasion?"

"Yeah, that's what I want to know, too, and why is Daddy home?" Zoey asked.

Taking the biscuits out of the oven, her mother answered, "Today is a big day for the Lyndon girls! Zoey, you have your Ohm's law presentation for the school science fair, and Jasmine has her audition for *The Sound of Music.*"

Her dad said, "I knew you'd need help carrying your stuff into school this morning. Plus, I wanted some of your mom's bacon," he said as he swiped a piece.

The family sat down to eat a nice big breakfast of bacon, eggs, potatoes, and biscuits. Both of the girls enjoyed the special breakfast that their mom had made for them and having their dad home.

"Thanks, Mom, for cooking this morning," Jasmine said as she gave her mom a hug.

"No problem, Jazz. This is one of the perks of working from home. I get the opportunity to fix my family a Saturday breakfast on a Tuesday." She smiled and hugged her back. "Give me a minute to grab my keys, and I'll take you to school if you'd like."

"Yeah, that would be great. I won't have to ride the bus this morning."

"Well, since your dad is taking Zoey to school today, that frees me up to be able to take you to school instead of dropping you off at the bus stop," she said.

Everyone headed out, and the girls wished each other good luck with their presentation and audition.

At school, Zoey's dad helped her carry her science project to the auditorium, which was where the science fair was going to be held. After securing her trifold poster board on the table and making sure her project was operational, her father told her he would be back later.

Zoey was so excited she could hardly focus on Mrs. P.'s reading lesson, even though she totally liked the dark-green belted dress with the tie at the neck that she was wearing. She was still happy that her mom had made them a special breakfast and that her dad was home and had brought her to school. She could feel it in her bones that today was going to be a great day. She smiled to herself and tried to focus on the reading lesson.

Somehow the morning seemed to fly by. Mrs. P. went over a reading lesson and a writing lesson, and they got to go to the library. Everyone loves library day.

"Looks like you knew what you wanted," Josh Hightower said, motioning to the book in Zoey's hand.

Nodding her head, she said, "Yeah, I have wanted to read *The Bridge to Terabithia* for a little while. What book did you check out?"

"It's just another book in the Percy Jackson series." Since they were the first two to find their books, they had to wait for the rest of the class to check out their books.

"What book did you get, Josh?" Olivia asked, standing entirely too close for his liking.

"Percy Jackson," he said flatly.

Mrs. P. noticed that Olivia had not checked out anything and suggested that she find something to read in class during her downtime. She rolled her eyes, making sure that Mrs. P. didn't catch her, and went to find a book.

When she was out of earshot, Josh turned to Zoey and said in exasperation, "She is such a pain!"

"It's pretty apparent that she likes you," Zoey said.

"Yeah, well, she's a flirt, and I like her ... not like that. I used to like her, but now she just flirts all the time, and it's annoying."

"Maybe you should tell her that it's bothering you."

"No, I don't want to hurt her feelings. Besides, I'm hoping that she'll eventually see that I'm not interested and leave me alone."

"I think you should say something, but I promise that I won't say anything."

Just then Mrs. P. told the students that it was time to check out. Once everyone had their books and checked them out, they returned to their classroom to drop off their books and get ready for lunch. The day had flown by, and it was already time for the science fair. Mrs. P. released the students who were participating so they could go to the auditorium and get set up. There would be judges who walked around to discuss each student's work.

When Zoey got to her project on the auditorium stage, she noticed that her father and mother were already seated in the first row. She ran over and gave them both a big hug. "I'm so glad that you made it," she said excitedly.

"Of course we made it, Zoe! I've been looking forward to this all day," her mother said with a genuine smile.

"I've checked out some of the other entries, and it looks like you have some stiff competition, baby girl," her father said as he looked at the other students' projects.

"Yeah, I know some of them are really interesting."

Tommi walked over to tell Zoey that the judges were starting to come around, and she needed to get back onstage. She said a quick hello to Zoey's parents before she and Zoey took their places on the stage.

Before long the auditorium was packed with students, teachers, parents, grandparents, and the judges. Zoey answered the judges' questions and showed them how her project worked, and she even got to use the laser pointer that her father had let her borrow. She was proud of the work she had done and was surprised that she wasn't nervous at all once the judges started asking her questions.

"How did it go?" Her father asked as he approached her table.

"I think it went okay." She beamed proudly.

"It looked like they were asking you a lot of questions."

"Yeah, they were, but I was able to answer them, and I got to use the laser pointer that you gave me a couple of times."

Laughing, her father told her, "Good for you! I'm glad you got a chance to use it," and he gave her a big hug.

Her mom looked over her project and told her that she should be proud of herself for all her hard work. They walked around and looked at the other science projects. Her parents wanted to say hello to Mrs. P. before they left.

"Hello, Mr. and Mrs. Lyndon," Mrs. P. said as she saw the Lyndon family approaching. She had just finished talking to another one of the fourth-grade teachers.

"Hello, Mrs. P.," the Lyndons replied in unison as they shook her hand.

"I hope you enjoyed the science fair. The children all did such an amazing job this year," she said, nearly bursting with pride for her students. "I was so impressed with Zoey's project on Ohm's law."

"Thank you," Mrs. Lyndon said. "She worked really hard on her project for weeks."

"And it shows!" Mrs. P. said.

"Zoey is an excellent student, and I enjoy having her in my class this year. She has really settled in nicely."

Another parent was waiting to speak with Mrs. P., so Mrs. Lyndon told her that she would reach out to her about volunteering soon and thanked her for her time.

When they got back to Zoey's table to pack up her project, she found a blue ribbon placed on the table next to her experiment.

"Oh my God!" she said as she picked up the ribbon. Both of her parents beamed with pride, congratulated her, and gave her hugs. She could not believe that she had won first place and couldn't wait to get home and tell Jasmine. On the car ride home, she was thinking that this was the best day ever!

Chapter 8

Winners

"Jasmine! Where are you?" Zoey yelled when they walked into the house.

"Upstairs," she yelled back.

Zoey flew up the steps to tell Jasmine all about the contest and to show her the blue ribbon.

Due to attending Zoey's school science fair, her mother decided that tonight would be a good night for Antonio's pizza. She ordered their usual two pizzas and had her husband go to pick them up.

At dinner, as they ate their pizza and the salad that their mom quickly threw together, the girls talked nonstop about their exciting day.

"I got the part of Maria in the school play!" Jasmine gleefully blurted.

"Congratulations, Jazz! I knew you would get a great part," both parents told her.

Reaching for a slice of pizza, her mom asked, "Isn't Maria the main character?"

"Yes, Mom, she is," Jasmine said.

"Oh, sweetie, I am so excited for you. I can't wait to see you in action."

"Do you know who's playing Captain von Trapp?" her mother asked.

Blushing and trying to hide a smile, Jasmine said, "Noah."

"Ooh ... the plot do thicken," teased Zoey.

Jasmine gave her sister the stink eye and told her mom, "Noah has a really nice voice and had the best audition out of all the boys."

"It would have been nice if the auditions had been open and we could have been there to support you," her mom said.

"That's okay, Mom. You and Dad would have probably just made me more nervous, so it's a good thing you weren't there," Jasmine said.

"Well I plan on being at every show once the play opens!" her father said, proudly raising his glass to her accomplishment. Everyone raised their glasses and toasted with a boisterous "Cheers!"

Zoey gave Jasmine a recap of the science fair and told her about some of the other science projects. The Lyndons finished up dinner, and Zoey and Jasmine had to clean up before they got started on their homework.

That night after Zoey got ready for bed, she went downstairs to say good night to her parents. When she entered the family room, she saw her father was resting his eyes in his usual spot on the sofa, and her mom was watching some show on TV eating a bowl of ice cream.

"Hey, Zoe. You all ready for bed?"

"Yes, Mom. I just came to say good night to you and Daddy."

Zoey's mom moved her feet off the ottoman and motioned for Zoey to have a seat. "You had a pretty exciting day," she said as she ate another spoonful of ice cream.

"Yeah." She smiled. "I can't wait to show Tommi and Josh Hightower my first-place ribbon. Do you mind if I take it to school tomorrow?"

"No, not at all. You earned it. You can show it to Mrs. P. too. She was so impressed with your project."

Zoey agreed and gave her a warm smile.

"You know, Zoe, it wasn't that long ago that you were super nervous about starting a new school, making new friends, and worrying about accidentally walking into the boys' bathroom."

Zoey laughed. "Yeah, I remember."

"You've made some good friends, and I'm proud of how you're learning to navigate and find your way."

"I know. Who knew that the Lou would end up being such a cool place to live?"

"The Lou?" her mom repeated, trying to figure out what her daughter was talking about.

Zoey laughed and said it was how people affectionately referred to Saint Louis. She then gave her mom a hug and a kiss good night and tapped her dad's shoulder to wake him up to give him a hug and kiss good night.

He opened his eyes and gave her a sleepy smile and said "Good night, baby girl."

As Zoey lay in bed that night, she replayed the events of the day in her mind with a little smile on her face. She was still reeling about coming in first place at the science fair. She was finding that fourth grade was not so bad, and even though she still missed her friends from back in Philly, she was also looking forward to all that she would discover in Saint Louis.

Zoey took a peek at the clock and saw that it was after 10:00 p.m. She turned over to get comfortable before finally drifting off to sleep.

About the Author

Micheal Anderson is an author who enjoys writing middle grade fiction and understands the value of representation in children's stories. She lives in St. Louis, Missouri with her husband and two daughters. Micheal enjoys blogging, jazz music and loves to travel abroad.

Please write a review

Authors love hearing from their readers!
Please let Micheal Anderson know what you
thought of *Zoey Lyndon's Big Move to the Lou*.

Leave a review on her website
everythingmicheal.com.

You can also leave a review on Amazon or
Goodreads and this will help other children
discover *Zoey Lyndon's Big Move to the Lou*.

Thank You!

CPSIA information can be obtained
at www.ICGtesting.com
Printed in the USA
LVHW040458300920
667478LV00007B/958